The Town Musicians of Bremen

Special Edition
2ⁿᵈ Edition 2013

Translation by Hildegard and David Skevington

Based on the Grimm Brothers' fairy tale
© EDITION TEMMEN 2010 – Hohenlohestraße 21 – 28209 Bremen – Tel. +49-421-34843-0
Fax +49-421-348094 – info@edition-temmen.de – www.edition-temmen.de
Production: EDITION TEMMEN – All rights reserved – ISBN 978-3-8378-7010-7
printed in Hong Kong

The Town Musicians
of Bremen

Illustrated and vividly re-told

by

EDITION TEMMEN

Once upon a time, a miller and a donkey lived together in a mill.

The donkey carried the sacks of corn from
the station to the mill. The miller ground
the corn, and the donkey carried
the sacks of flour from the mill
back to the station.

Day in and day out it was the same and the donkey did his work tirelessly.

But when the donkey grew old, and carrying the loads had become too much of an effort, the miller said to him: "Go and look for another place to stay, you old thing, you are no use to me anymore!" And he chased the donkey away.

This really suited the donkey and he set off for
Bremen because he had always wanted to go
there and become a musician. So the donkey went
on his way and cheerfully pranced along the road
towards Bremen.

After all, it wasn't far to Bremen and the donkey saw everything there was to be seen along the way.

He came upon a dog sitting near a river, sobbing silently and clearly grief-stricken.
"Why are you crying, you poor creature, is life not amusing enough for you?"
   "Oh," moaned the dog, "how could it be amusing? I'm old, I can't catch hares any more and my master has chased me away."
      "Well," the donkey exclaimed, "I can tell from your voice that you are highly musical. Come with me to Bremen and together we'll make music there."

That suited the old dog, as indeed he loved music above all else and most of all he loved the saxophone. How often during the long lonely nights had he played his saxophone to the full moon!

And so he joined the donkey on the road to
Bremen. With the dog perched on top of
the donkey.
Soon they came upon a cat sitting in
the middle of the road, not looking
too happy.

"Oh dear, old moggy, what's the matter with you? You look like a hundred rainy days. What happened to you, you poor thing?"

"Just because I no longer bring home any mice," the cat wailed, "my mistress has chased me away."

"So what?" the donkey exclaimed, "forget about your mistress, come to Bremen with us. We're going to make music there, and you can sing, can't you?"

"Oh yes, like a canary, whenever the moon shines in the sky," the cat replied and started meowing.

"There you are," the donkey nodded, "that sounds like Brahms played on a violin. The people of Bremen are very good at heart, they will reward us generously."

And so the cat joined them on the road to Bremen.

BREMEN

And just then, they came across old rooster Gustl Hannemann sitting on a gatepost crowing miserably.

"Oh," the donkey exclaimed, "if you are in such a bad state, why not come with us to Bremen.

We are musicians. You only have to squeal like a saw, young people love that."
So, the rooster too joined them on the road to Bremen making four in all: the donkey, the dog, the cat, and the rooster flying above.

But eventually darkness overtook them and they had to look for a place to sleep. The donkey and the dog stayed under a tree, the cat climbed onto the branches and rooster Hannemann flew high up onto the tree-top and crowed: "Do come up here, boys and girls, I can see a light in the distance! That could be a lodging house."

So the donkey climbed to the top of the tree, the rooster settled himself comfortably on the soft cat because he was tired and the dog looked up and barked: "What do you see there, donkey?"

"A house," the donkey shouted, "it must
be a lodging house, maybe there is a
warm bed for each of us ..."

"Then let's go there," barked the dog and they set off at once in the dark.
After a while they reached the house, but it was not a lodging house, it was a robbers' lair!
The windows were brightly lit as if it was Christmas and inside the robbers were making a mighty din.

The donkey looked through the window and the cat asked: "What do you see, old grey coat? Tell us!"

"A richly-laid table with the best food in the world," the donkey exclaimed, "and a few robbers."

And he climbed down the short ladder.
"That would be just the thing for us, wouldn't it?"
the dog said. "Is there a bit of sausage there, too?"

And so they deliberated how to get the robbers out of the house. The bold rooster said: "We'll storm in just like hussars and take possession of the house!"

So they climbed
onto the windowsill
and burst into the
room shouting and
screaming.

And the robbers took flight
from the house as if chased
by a pack of hounds.

When the robbers had left
the house, the four friends
enjoyed a fine feast stuffing
themselves with all the food.

After the feast they each
looked for a comfortable
place to settle and then
switched off the light.

When the robbers saw from a distance
that it had become dark in the house,
their leader said: "We shouldn't have let
ourselves be tricked. Go back and see what's
happening, Robber Gregor!"
So Robber Gregor crept
softly back to the house.

The robber found everything quiet. But two sparks were glowing by the stove and when he tried to put a match to them they turned out to be the glowing eyes of the cat and it jumped into the robber's face like the devil Lucifer himself!

The robber wanted to run from the house, but when he came past the sofa, the dog was lying there. It nipped him in the calves as if biting into a sausage, and the robber raced out of the door ...

First he stumbled over a pitch fork, then the donkey kicked him in the backside with his hind leg, the rooster shrieked from the roof "Cock-a-doodle-doooooo!" and

Robber Gregor ran like a hare back to his
comrades. There he reported to the leader:
"There was a glowing dragon sitting
in the kitchen and it struck me

in the face with its claws until sparks were flying.
An enormous bagpipe was sleeping
on the sofa,

it howled at me and dug itself right into my calves. And I can't even begin to describe what happened after that, it was so terrible."

So the robbers went away.

The musicians liked the house so much that they decided to make it their home. Only when they needed a little money did they go to Bremen to make music in the market-place.
At a guess it was seven kilometres – as the crow flies!
That wasn't so bad!
They could manage that!
Don't you think?